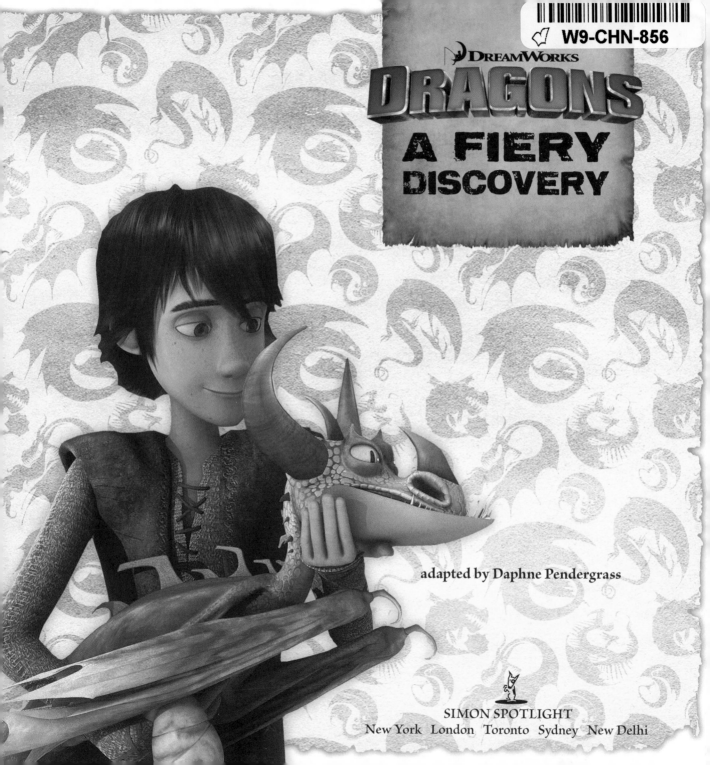

DREAMWORKS
DRAGONS
A FIERY DISCOVERY

adapted by Daphne Pendergrass

SIMON SPOTLIGHT
New York London Toronto Sydney New Delhi

SIMON SPOTLIGHT
An imprint of Simon & Schuster Children's Publishing Division
1230 Avenue of the Americas, New York, New York 10020
This Simon Spotlight edition June 2015

SIMON SPOTLIGHT and colophon are registered trademarks of Simon & Schuster, Inc.
For information about special discounts for bulk purchases, please contact Simon & Schuster Special Sales
at 1-866-506-1949 or business@simonandschuster.com.
Manufactured in the United States of America 0615 LAK
1 2 3 4 5 6 7 8 9 10
ISBN 978-1-4814-4815-4
ISBN 978-1-4814-2769-2 (eBook)

The dragon riders were practicing flying in the woods one day when Astrid and Stormfly neared a cluster of trees.

"Stormfly, up!" Astrid shouted. But at the last minute, Stormfly ducked under the branches instead of going over them.

"You were right," Astrid said as she patted her dragon. One of the things Hiccup and his friends had learned about dragons was that sometimes a dragon knows the best way to go, even when its rider doesn't.

Just then a whirring fireball flew by their heads. When it landed, Hiccup saw that it was a dragon—a dragon he had never encountered before!

"Hey, little guy. Who are you?" Hiccup asked as he coaxed the dragon out of its hiding place.

Toothless growled and tried to stop Hiccup, but his rider scooped up the smaller dragon and headed back to Berk.

At the Berk Dragon Training Academy, everyone was curious about the new dragon. "It's a whole new species!" said Fishlegs excitedly. "There's no telling what it might do."

"Well, somebody's got to take him home," Astrid added. She and the others immediately took a step back from Hiccup and the little dragon.

"Well, big guy, here's your somebody," Hiccup said, picking up the dragon.

The mysterious dragon quickly made himself at home in Stoick and Hiccup's house. When Stoick asked Toothless to light the fire, the little dragon shot out a burst of flame before Toothless could.

"Looks like you got torched!" Stoick said. "Oh, that's his name by the way: Torch!"

Toothless growled suspiciously.

Then Hiccup put out Toothless' food, but Torch ate it all when Hiccup wasn't looking! And at bedtime, Torch took Toothless' bed.

"Toothless, you don't mind sharing your bed for the night, do you?" Hiccup asked.

But Toothless was mad. He flew into the rafters over Hiccup's bed and kept an eye on Torch all night.

The next morning at the Academy, Hiccup and the others measured and observed this new species.

"Twenty inches for the wings," Astrid said.

Then Fishlegs administered the Eel Reaction Test. Torch was the only dragon known to Vikings who wasn't afraid of eels!

Hiccup wanted Toothless to show Torch how to fly, but Toothless wouldn't budge.

Then Torch did something amazing—he flapped his wings and sparks came out of his mouth. He flew around and around the arena, etching a burn mark onto the ground.

"It spun like, like a typhoon!" Fishlegs cried.

"And he came back, just like a boomerang," said Astrid.

So they decided to name the new species the Typhoomerang.

That night, as Hiccup was adding a Typhoomerang chapter to the *Book of Dragons*, Torch and Toothless got into a fight. Torch spit a fireball at Toothless, setting Hiccup's bedroom on fire!

But Hiccup thought that Toothless had started the fire. "What is wrong with you?" he shouted as Toothless ran off.

Toothless was sad that Hiccup wasn't listening to him. He went to the forest to be alone, but there he found a massive Typhoomerang with her two babies, who looked just like Torch.

That's when Toothless realized that Torch wasn't lost at all—he was just separated from his mother. Toothless had to warn Hiccup before Torch's mom came looking for her baby!

Back in the village, Hiccup was worried about Toothless, so he went to talk to Gobber. "It's like Toothless is jealous," he said.

"Something must be going on under the surface. Dragons are complex creatures," Gobber replied.

Suddenly, Toothless came roaring into Gobber's shop, trying to warn Hiccup about the mother Typhoomerang. He picked up Torch and tried flying off toward the forest.

"Back down," Hiccup yelled, putting himself between the two dragons.

Hiccup needed to get Toothless away from Torch, so he tried riding him to the cove. But Toothless flew toward the forest, trying to find Torch's mother.

That only made Hiccup angrier. "Where are you going?" he shouted.

Hiccup turned Toothless around and landed him in a canyon. "You've got to stay here," Hiccup said. "I've got to separate you two until I can figure this out."

Then he climbed out of the canyon, leaving Toothless alone.

When Hiccup got back to the Academy, Astrid tried comforting him. "You did the right thing with Toothless," she said. "He'll snap out of it."

Tuffnut interrupted them as he and Ruffnut entered the arena. "You guys would not believe what we just saw in the forest."

"The whole thing was *torched,*" Ruffnut added.

"Torched?" said Hiccup slowly. The riders all looked at the little dragon in Hiccup's arms. Then they headed to the woods.

When they flew over the forest, Hiccup was shocked to see the same burn mark that Torch had made, only much bigger. Then the riders saw something even more terrifying—a giant Typhoomerang flying through the sky!

"That's Torch's mother," said Hiccup.

"Torch is a baby!" Astrid said in awe.

"That's what Toothless was trying to tell me . . . ," Hiccup said.

But Toothless' warning came a little too late—the mother Typhoomerang spotted Hiccup holding Torch and swooped in toward him!

The other riders scattered. Hiccup set down Torch and ran to the canyon where he had left Toothless.

Hiccup found his Night Fury just in time, and together they flew away from the mother Typhoomerang.

"I'm so sorry," Hiccup said to Toothless. "I should've listened to you."

But there was no time for apologies; Torch's mother was right on their tail. And Torch wouldn't go back to her—he was still clinging to Hiccup!

Hiccup saw that trying to outfly the mother wasn't going to work. "Toothless, up!" he called. "Now, dive!"

The mother Typhoomerang followed them, and when they dove back to the ground, she lost her balance and landed hard on the forest floor. But when she shook off the fall, she saw that Torch was safe. The baby dragon leaped off Toothless and started playing with his siblings.

"Good job, bud," Hiccup said, patting Toothless's head. "Everybody's back where they belong." Hiccup waved good-bye as the mother Typhoomerang lifted Torch back onto her wing and took off, raining a spinning shower of sparks down on them.

Hiccup and Toothless soared home across the sky.

"I should've known you were just trying to protect me. That's what you do," Hiccup said. He learned an important lesson that day—sometimes what your dragon is trying to say is what you really need to hear.